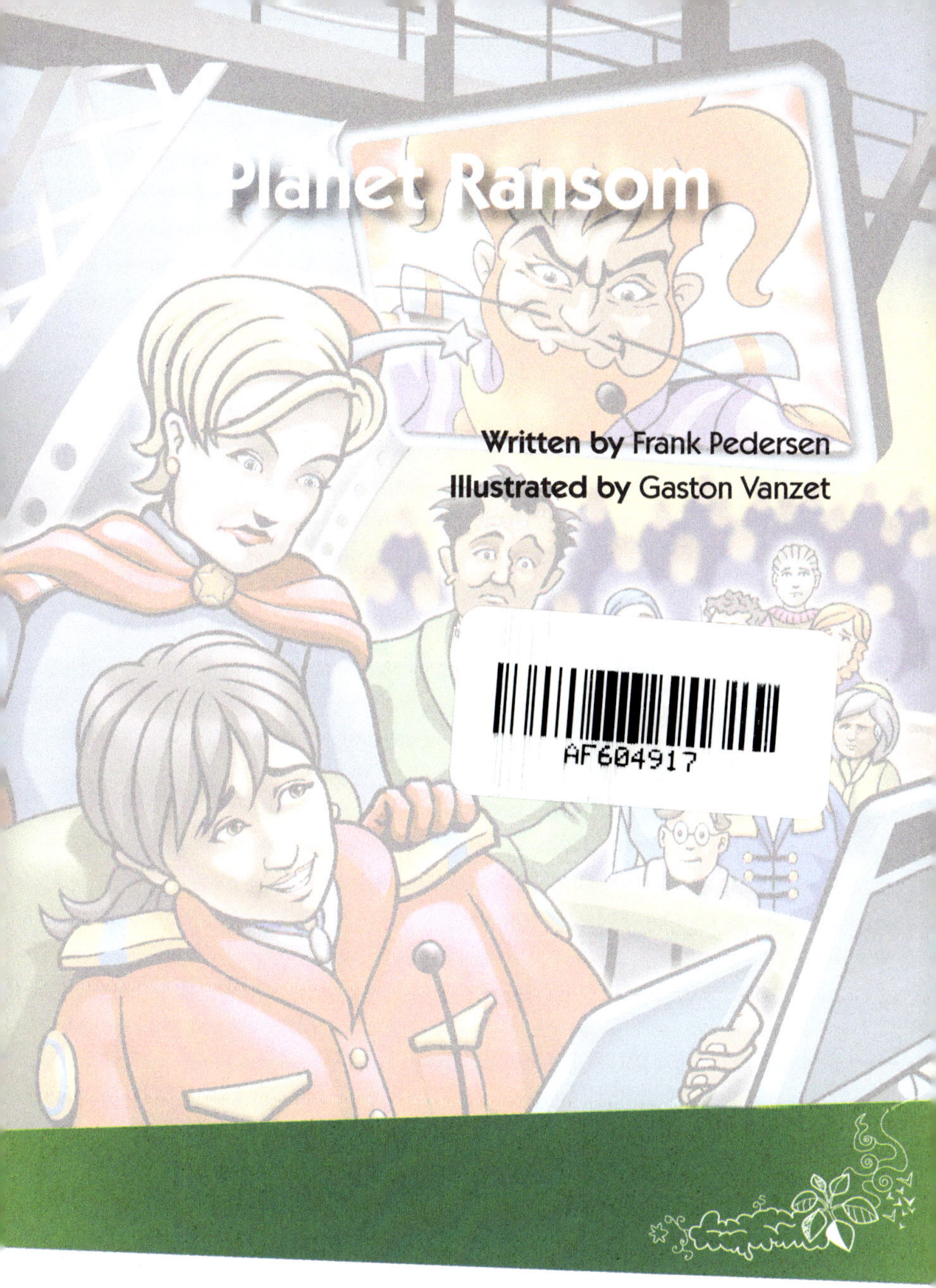

Planet Ransom

Written by Frank Pedersen
Illustrated by Gaston Vanzet

Meet the Characters

Mila Shovetzka

A Russian space scientist.

Dr Xerxes

A mad scientist.

President Sternov

The Russian president.

Rosco Fortescue

A greedy billionaire.

Dear Reader

With over 2 billion people connected to the Internet, the information you can quickly find online is amazing. I was surfing the Internet one day, when suddenly I thought, "What could humans achieve if

everybody online worked together on a project?"

I guess it would depend on who was in charge!

Frank Pedersen

Author

The Solar System

1. The Sun 2. Earth 3. Mars

(Distances are not to scale.)

LOCATION: MARS 10.00 am, 21 FEBRUARY

The room fell silent. No one dared breathe. Every one of the hundred Mars council members gazed at their notes or looked at their shoes.

The only sounds were the footsteps of the evil Dr Xerxes, as he strode towards the lectern. Grasping its edges with thin, bony fingers, he glared at the council. An icy chill fell over the room.

Dr Xerxes ran a hand through his wild mane of flaming red hair. He basked in the silent fear that rose like an invisible cloud from the room. Then the president of Xerxes City, humankind's first space colony, shouted the first terrifying word of his speech. Every eye in the room was fixed upon him.

Travelling at the speed of light, the images of the meeting on Mars sped towards the huge screens in the space centre in Moscow.

Until the first images arrived, the people there saw nothing but dark static.

"What's happening?" growled President Elenya Sternov, Earth's most powerful leader. "Why is it taking so long?"

Mila Shovetzka, the scientist in charge of the space centre, turned in her chair.

"Mars and Earth travel around the Sun in elliptical orbits," she said. "At their furthest point, they are over 400 million kilometres apart. Right now, they are at nearly their closest point – but that's still a distance of 58 million kilometres. From that far, signals from Mars take 193 seconds to reach Earth."

President Sternov scowled at Mila.

Specks of light danced across the screen. Three and a quarter minutes later, an image of Dr Xerxes burst on the screen.

His wild eyes transfixed those watching on Mars and on Earth.

"Annihilation!" he shouted.

Across the vastness of space, a cold fear gripped the people of two tiny planets.

LOCATION: MOSCOW JAIL 10.04 am, 21 FEBRUARY

In a grey, dimly lit cell in Moscow's worst jail, Rosco Fortescue paced up and down. Outside, a blizzard raged. For weeks, only the brave had gone out into the icy storm. Now and again, a heavy truck rumbled by. The walls of the cell shook with the noise.

Rosco Fortescue was not alone in trying to shake off the chill that ate at his bones.

R Fort

Millions of people in the Northern Hemisphere were seeing the worst blizzards for a century.

In contrast, those who lived in the Southern Hemisphere were sweltering under a long drought. Around the planet, food crops were poor. Power and energy systems were breaking down.

Once a billionaire, Rosco Fortescue had run many of Earth's food and power companies. But those companies had also depleted Earth's resources and polluted its atmosphere. When Mars had first been colonised, he had been too greedy and had fallen foul of President Sternov and Dr Xerxes.

Now he was in jail. Now, Earth and its people were in crisis.

Dr Xerxes waited for his first word to sink in.

"Annihilation," he growled. "That is what we face unless we meet our greatest challenge."

Dr Xerxes stabbed a bony finger at his audience. "Earth is dying – and with it, we will die too. Unless we use every skill, all our knowledge and all our technology to design a solution."

The council of Xerxes City sat transfixed. Every one of them knew that Mars needed supplies from Earth. Without them, they knew that every human on Mars was doomed, too.

"I am the greatest scientist in this solar system," declared Dr Xerxes. He stared at the audience. "And I alone can save you. On Mars and on Earth, you must agree to my plans or ..."

An evil smile crossed Dr Xerxes' evil face. His bony fingers shook. His words struck fear into the hearts of those on Mars. At the same instant, his words began the long journey to Earth.

"He is mad," said Mila. "Mad and evil."

Dr Xerxes' words had created an uproar in Moscow. President Sternov was in a rage. The other scientists and leaders argued about what Dr Xerxes had said. But, as everyone knew, there was one fact that no one wanted to admit.

Dr Xerxes was right.

LOCATION: MOSCOW JAIL 6.00 am, 3 MARCH

Heavy footsteps echoed along a passage of the jail. Rosco Fortescue listened as they grew closer and stopped. A key scraped in the lock of his steel door.

"Rosco Fortescue," said the guard. "You have a phone call."

Rosco reached for the guard's mobile phone. The guard walked back down the passage.

Rosco stared at the number on the phone's screen. He lifted the phone to his ear. He was about to speak when he realised something.

The guard had left the door to his cell open.

"All our scientists agree we have, at best, ten years left," started Mila. She looked around the meeting. President Sternov was there, smiling like a snow leopard. Sitting next to her was Rosco Fortescue. He was clearly back in a position of power. Behind them sat Earth's leading scientists, designers, engineers and computer experts. Above all of them, Dr Xerxes watched from a huge screen.

"This is Dr Xerxes," said Mila, gritting her teeth. "And this is his plan."

She continued, “In five years, we will use all of Earth’s skills and knowledge. We will design and build humankind’s largest project – a ‘space ark’.”

The audience gasped. President Sternov and Rosco Fortescue nodded.

“We will build a new artificial planet,” said Mila. “We will link every computer in the world. We will ask every human on the planet to help us. We will use every scrap of data from the last thousand years. It will be the biggest – and the most important – project ever. We will use the skills, experience and knowledge of seven billion human beings for one aim. Survival. And we will start today.”

President Sternov rose to her feet.

"Earth Two will succeed," said the president. The tone of her voice made it clear this was an order. "It will be big enough for a billion people. Rosco Fortescue has put his companies at my ... I mean our ... disposal. And you, ladies and gentlemen, will work out all the details of our new planet." The president's eyes narrowed. Her voice was as cold as the blizzard raging outside.

"You have only five years. Why are you still here?"

The room emptied. Only the giant face of Dr Xerxes was left to stare out onto the desks and chairs. Three and a quarter minutes after Mila started speaking, the first images reached Mars. Dr Xerxes nodded. Three and a quarter minutes later, that image reached Earth.

But no one on Earth saw his face. The meeting to start Earth Two had begun and finished in less time than it took a beam of light to travel from Earth to Mars and back.

Mila hated her weekly meetings with President Sternov. Even when she was in a good mood, Elenya Sternov was like a carnivore.

"How does that old proverb go?" Mila thought. "If you can see the teeth of a lion, it may not be smiling at you."

Mila looked at her list. She took a deep breath.

"Behavioural and social sciences. Biochemistry. Botany. Chemistry. Computer science. Earth and space sciences. Engineering. Environmental sciences. Mathematics. Medicine and health. Microbiology. Physics. Zoology," she read. So many scientific areas. Could they ever work together? Mila turned the page.

"Then we have to think of architecture. Industrial design. Visual arts. Decorative arts. We can't simply live in a big machine. We're humans, not robots. Earth Two has to be home to many cultures."

There was a knock on the door. Rosco Fortescue came in. President Sternov had put him in charge of the project. That meant he was now Mila's boss. It didn't mean that she had to like him. She didn't.

"President Sternov. Miss Shovetzka," he said. President Sternov waved at a chair. Fortescue sat down.

"It has been one month since the start of Earth Two. People are sending in ideas and designs for every part of our new planet. Our Moscow supercomputers add every idea into one master design within seconds. Humankind's greatest plan is now underway."

"Good work, Rosco," said the president. Mila glanced across at him. Out of the trillions of megabytes of data being put together, she knew he had not contributed one single byte.

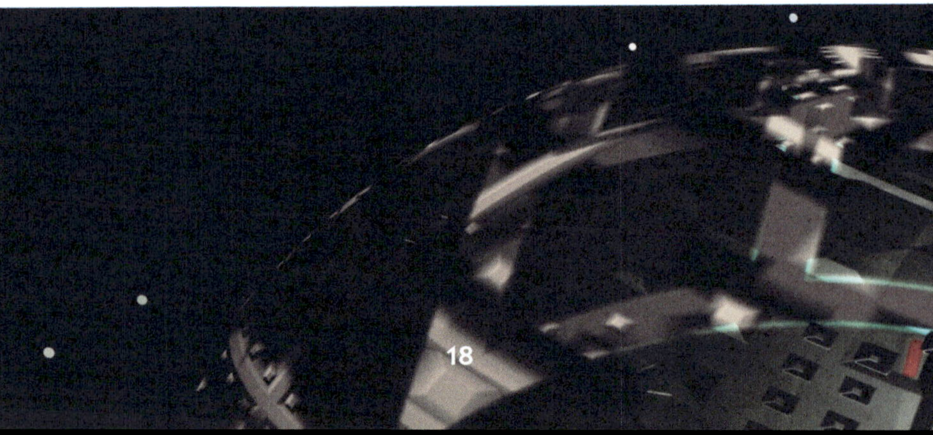

"Is this data secure?" asked President Sternov.

"Only three people will have a password to access it," replied Fortescue. The president nodded. She turned to Mila.

"Miss Shovetzka, Mr Fortescue and I have some vital business to discuss," said President Sternov. "Are there any more questions?"

Mila hesitated. There was a nagging thought at the back of her mind. Was this the time to bring it up?

"Well?" barked the president. "Do you have a question? Hurry up."

Mila took a deep breath.

"At our first meeting to discuss Earth Two, you said the new planet would be big enough for a billion people."

"Yes," snapped President Sternov. "What's your point?"

"Well, Earth has seven billion people, Madam President. I'm wondering ..."

Mila's voice trailed off. An icy glare from Sternov told her the conversation was over. Mila's fears were confirmed. Six billion people would be left on a dying planet.

Dr Xerxes gazed out of the window. Xerxes City was covered in domes, where humans, plants and animals could live. The city glowed like a handful of pearls scattered across the Martian surface.

The link between Earth and Mars burst into life. Dr Xerxes turned his eyes towards the computer. An image of President Sternov and Rosco Fortescue flashed across the screen.

Rosco Fortescue spoke.

"Dr Xerxes, as we have secretly agreed, Earth Two will only be big enough for 999 human beings, not a billion. That way, we can build it well ahead of our five-year date. Each of us will choose 333 people, including ourselves, to board Earth Two when it is complete."

"Dr Xerxes," said the president. "Designs for Earth Two are taking shape. As we agreed, only we three will see the designs. Each of us will have a password that we will share. That way, we can be sure of three things. Firstly, no one else will know the true size of Earth Two. Secondly, there will be no secrets amongst us. Thirdly, all three of us will have access to the same designs."

President Sternov paused.

"My password is DESPIC456. Rosco Fortescue's is TRAIT037. What will yours be?"

The images of President Sternov and Rosco Fortescue stared at Dr Xerxes. The evil scientist looked across the Martian landscape. He thought about his password. Secretly, he wanted to steal the plans and choose every one of the people on Earth Two himself. He laughed cruelly. He turned back to the screen.

"XERXES999," he replied.

LOCATION: MOSCOW PALACE 10.31 am, 1 MAY

President Sternov tapped the screen impatiently. The image of Dr Xerxes stood motionless before her and Fortescue. His evil eyes stared at them.

"Why is this taking so long?" she hissed to Fortescue.

Rosco Fortescue was about to reply, but President Sternov had had enough. She was used to instant answers. She jabbed at a key on her computer and stood up.

"I've put him on 'record'," she said. "I don't have time for this. I want to see this supercomputer for myself."

Rosco rose to his feet. He knew that if he didn't follow orders, he would find himself back in a cell. He followed President Sternov, who was muttering something about the speed of light.

The lift doors opened. "Ground floor," said a smooth recorded voice.

Mila stood looking at the exit to the palace. Outside, the storm was still dumping metres of snow onto the streets. Mila shivered, but it wasn't because of the weather.

"It's just not right," she said to herself. "How can they betray billions of people who think they are giving their ideas so they can all survive?"

"Ground floor," repeated the voice.

Mila stayed in the lift. She knew what she had to do. She hit the lift button again. The doors slid shut.

"Going up," said the voice. "Top floor."

LOCATION: MOSCOW PALACE . 10.32 am, 1 MAY

Sternov and Fortescue stood by the row of lifts. A green light lit up above one of the lifts. The pair strode inside.

"Going down," said the voice. "Basement carpark."

LOCATION: MOSCOW PALACE . 10.33 am, 1 MAY

Mila practised her speech on the way up.

"President Sternov, I will use all my powers to stop this plan," she said. The doors of Mila's lift opened. She summoned up all her courage. She strode towards Sternov's office. She knocked and walked in with her head held high.

"President Sternov, I will use ..."

Mila stopped. The room was empty, except for an image on a computer screen. It was Dr Xerxes. There was no sign of Sternov or Fortescue.

Suddenly, Dr Xerxes' evil laugh filled the empty office.

"XERXES999," he said.

Mila backed out of the office. She knew that if she was caught there, she would be in big trouble. She hurried towards the lifts, wondering what it was that she had just heard, three and a quarter minutes after it had been said on Mars.

LOCATION: MARS 10.34 am, 1 MAY

Dr Xerxes jabbed a key on his computer with a bony finger. The link with Earth was broken. He had work to do. Part of the plan for Earth Two was to build a giant spaceport to take people from Mars to their new artificial home. That would require almost as much technology as it would take to build Earth Two itself. Dr Xerxes was counting on that.

"Once everything arrives, I will steal the plans for Earth Two. I will build it myself, here on Mars," he said to himself. "Except it won't be called Earth Two. The future of the human race will depend on ..."

He grinned excitedly.

"Planet Xerxes!"

If there had been any air on Mars, an evil laugh would have echoed across Xerxes City. Instead, it just grew louder within the walls of an office, high above the Martian landscape.

LOCATION: SPACE CENTRE 10.00 am, 13 JUNE

"It just isn't right," protested Mila. Her old teacher, Professor Pierre, sipped his mug of tea.

"If what you say is correct, then this will not only be the biggest project humans have ever done," he said, "it will also be the biggest deception."

"The computers have been using people's ideas, designing Earth Two for months," she said. "There will be thousands of carefully drawn plans, using every idea people have sent from around the globe."

"If people saw those plans, they might realise what's going on," said Professor Pierre. "Do you have access to the supercomputers?"

"Yes, I do," replied Mila. "But I will make three enemies if I release the plans."

Professor Pierre took another sip of his tea.

"You will make six billion enemies if you don't," he replied.

LOCATION: MOSCOW 10.30 am, 13 JUNE

Rosco took his VIP seat on the space liner that was about to depart for Mars. It would take the space liner 60 days to arrive at Mars.

He knew that President Sternov did not trust Dr Xerxes. When she had asked him to travel to Mars to check on the building of the spaceport, he had quickly agreed. He was tired of the snow in Moscow.

The idea of two months in a VIP cabin was very attractive. It reminded him of the days when he was a billionaire and flew from city to city in his private jet.

"Those were the days," he smiled. He relaxed into the soft VIP seat. The rumble of the engines grew louder as the space liner began its launch.

"This is much better than the rumble of trucks driving over my cell," he smiled.

LOCATION: MOSCOW PALACE 10.35 am, 13 JUNE

From her window in the palace, Elenya Sternov saw a distant white streak disappear into the clouds. Even from a hundred kilometres away, the vapour trail left by the space liner heading to Mars was visible.

She went back to her desk. One of the two other people who had access to Earth Two's designs was on a gloomy planet millions of kilometres away. Now, the second was on board a space liner for two months.

She tapped her computer. She too had plans of her own. They did not include Dr Xerxes or Fortescue. They did involve 998 of her own friends, however – plus Elenya Sternov.

At the space centre, Mila Shovetzka logged onto the computer. She quickly found what she was looking for. She double-clicked on the folder called Earth Two and waited. In the folder, there would be huge files. She expected it would take some time for them to come up on screen.

What she hadn't expected was the screen that came up next.

"Password," demanded the supercomputer. "This is a secret folder."

Mila sat back in her chair, deflated. She had no idea of the password. She racked her brains for something that President Sternov, Rosco Fortescue or Dr Xerxes might use.

She typed in President Sternov's birthday. That was a public holiday in Russia. Everybody knew that date.

17082001

The "waiting" icon appeared on her screen as the supercomputer tried the password she had typed in.

"Password," demanded the supercomputer again. "This is a secret folder."

"Blast!" said Mila. It wasn't the president's birthday. She tapped in "RF-BILLIONAIRE." Everyone knew that was how Rosco Fortescue liked to be known.

RF-BILLIONAIRE

Again, she watched the "waiting" icon. Again, the same screen appeared.

"Password," demanded the supercomputer. "This is a secret folder."

Mila wondered what Dr Xerxes would use. She had no idea when his birthday was or ...

Mila's memory flashed back a month and a half. Wait! Could that be it?

Trembling, she reached for the keyboard and started to type.

Again, Mila Shovetzka watched the "waiting" icon anxiously.

Nearly two weeks passed. By now, the space liner Rosco Fortescue was on would be too far into its journey to make a return to Earth. With every hour, Earth's orbit around the Sun took it another 100 000 kilometres further away.

It was time for President Sternov to put her plan into action. She logged on to the supercomputer. She found the folder she wanted to open. Another screen came up.

"Password," demanded the supercomputer. "This is a secret folder."

"It'll be even more secret once I've finished with it," said President Sternov grimly. She typed in a password – not her password, but the one used by Rosco Fortescue. "TRAIT037."

That way, anyone tracking who had opened the folder would see only that Rosco Fortescue had opened it, not President Sternov.

"Access granted," said the supercomputer. "Loading files."

President Sternov rubbed her hands together. She could hardly wait to see for herself the plans that were being drawn up by seven billion humans, all working together for one thing.

"Providing an escape planet for me and my closest advisors," said President Sternov.

Finally, the folder opened. When President Sternov saw what was inside, her eyes widened.

Her mouth dropped open. Her face turned as white as the snowdrifts banking up against the palace. And then her surprise turned to a rage, hotter than the furnaces that supplied heat, energy and clouds of pollution to Moscow.

LOCATION: MOSCOW PALACE 10.00 am, 28 JUNE

Mila stood in the lift carrying her to the top floor. She hated her weekly meetings with President Sternov. She was especially not looking forward to this one.

She had no idea whether the president had discovered what was inside the Earth Two folder. If President Elenya Sternov had the personality of a carnivore on a good day, there was no telling what she would do on a bad day.

The lift doors opened.

"Top floor," said a recorded voice.

Mila stepped out. She walked towards the president's office and knocked.

"Miss Shovetzka," said President Sternov, waving her inside. Mila watched her face closely. It was difficult to tell with President Sternov whether you were about to get a promotion or a grey, dimly lit cell.

President Sternov fixed Mila with a steely gaze.

"You are in control of our space centre. Do you have a password for secret folders on the supercomputer?"

"No," replied Mila truthfully. She didn't have a password – but she knew someone else's.

"I didn't think so," the president carried on. "I'm afraid we have a problem. A serious problem."

Mila swallowed. Her head filled with images of the damp cells that lay behind the walls of Moscow's high security jail.

"All the designs that the supercomputer has for Earth Two have gone," said President Sternov. "All of them, deleted."

Mila's heart was pounding so hard she was sure the president would be able to hear it.

"And I know who the culprit is," snarled President Sternov. Her angry eyes met Mila's.

"Dr Xerxes," she hissed. "I looked up the access files to see who had last logged into the super computer. Dr Xerxes had used his password to open the secret folder."

"I ... I ..." began Mila.

President Sternov ignored her.

"We need another plan urgently," continued the president. "This is a disaster. If seven billion people find that all their work to escape from a doomed planet has gone, the consequences will be unthinkable."

President Sternov looked at Mila with a look that reminded her of a crocodile feeling sorry for itself.

"All those poor people," said President Sternov. "Imagine how they'll feel when they discover there is no hope for them."

Mila desperately wanted to say, "Exactly the same way six billion of them would have felt when they found out how many places there really were on Earth Two." But she didn't.

She had a far better speech prepared. She was about to offer President Sternov the chance to become a hero.

LOCATION: MARS 10.32 am, 28 JUNE

On Mars, Dr Xerxes was angry. His eyes looked like they were about to explode.

"You traitor!" he roared, staring at the empty Earth Two folder on his computer screen. He saw the last password used to log in. He knew exactly who that belonged to. Rosco had cheated him once again! He let out a roar.

"Just wait until that space liner lands here," he breathed in a terrifying growl.

LOCATION: MOSCOW PALACE 11.30 am, 1 JULY

In Moscow's frozen palace grounds, President Sternov smiled into the TV cameras.

"I have great news!" she said. "The problems facing Earth are countless. But, this morning, I have decided we will not be leaving our home planet.

"The past months have shown that we can work together as one group of seven billion people," continued the president. "And with seven billion human beings using all their skills and ideas, there is no problem that we cannot solve.

“We humans are successful because we face challenges, we don’t run away from them. And that is what we will do now. We will work together to fix the problems so that everyone can stay on Earth.”

President Sternov smiled into the cameras. She knew that people around the world were being inspired by her words of courage. No one need know that the president’s secret plans had changed. No one need know that someone else with courage had already used those words three days before.

"We will link every computer to enlist the brains and creativity of every human. We will use every scrap of data we have discovered to solve our global problems. It will be the most gargantuan – and the most important – project that humans have ever undertaken. We will use the skills of seven billion human beings all working together for one aim: helping our planet survive. We will start today. And we will succeed."

LOCATION: SPACE CENTRE 11.31 am, 1 JULY

Back at the space centre, Mila was watching the TV. She smiled at Professor Pierre.

"That woman does have some great ideas," smiled the professor, switching the TV off. "Just like someone else I know."

Mila laughed.

"Soon, she'll be able to use seven billion ideas," she said. "If they allow us to survive on our planet, everyone will be happy."

"I wonder if anyone copied those plans for Earth Two before they deleted them?" said Professor Pierre. "Once we've saved Earth, the idea of sending President Sternov, Dr Xerxes, Rosco Fortescue and all their friends into space sounds quite appealing."

"Maybe they did, maybe they didn't," replied Mila innocently. "Who knows?"